# Planting A Seed Of Faith

## Nevada Lister-Kassa

iUniverse, Inc.
New York Bloomington

# Planting A Seed Of Faith

*iUniverse books may be ordered through booksellers or by contacting:*

*iUniverse
1663 Liberty Drive
Bloomington, IN 47403
www.iuniverse.com
1-800-Authors (1-800-288-4677)*

*Because of the dynamic nature of the Internet, any Web addresses or
links contained in this book may have changed since publication and may
no longer be valid.*

*ISBN: 978-1-4401-8534-2 (sc)
ISBN: 978-1-4401-8535-9 (ebk)*

*Printed in the United States of America*

*iUniverse rev. date: 12/03/2009*

*This book is dedicated to*

The Lord and Savior Jesus Christ
My Children, Grandchildren, Great grandchildren
My Brothers and Sisters

# *Introduction*

One thing I have learned over the years is God has whatever we need. He can solve any problem whether large or small. The thing I like most about God's problem solving is that he is fair to all concerned. We as human beings are naturally self-centered. When we hurt we want everyone to hurt. When we are happy we want everyone to be happy. It doesn't always work out like that.

Some years ago I was going through several crises in my life at the same time. Because I was so depressed people kind of stayed away from me. When you are going through something you will learn fast who your true friends are and usually it's not the people you thought it would be. A friend I had known for years came to me and said have you given these problems to God? I said no. She said you have to plant a seed of faith. I said ok I don't know why I didn't think of that. I had no idea what she was talking about and I did not want her to know. I thought on planting a seed of faith for a week and could not figure out what she was talking about or how to do it. I heard someone on TV talking about faith seeding. This had to do with giving money into a ministry. I went to the bible and looked up scriptures on faith and seed planting. Finally I cried out in my distress, God help me understand what she was talking about. When you cry out to God honestly for knowledge he will give it to you. So be prepared to receive.

I was in a deep sleep a few weeks later; I dreamed a deep powerful voice was teaching me about faith and how it works. The teacher gave me a scenario of a newly planted seed in a field. That is how I came about the 5 phases discussed in this book. I planted a seed of faith, through prayer, for each of the problems I was experiencing. For the first time in my life I was able to stay out of the problems and let God handle them. Each problem was resolved by God in his own time and according to his will and they worked out for the good of all involved.

1. Remember for your prayers to be answered:
    a)  Ask for what you want or need.
    b)  Have strong faith that you will receive.
    c)  Act upon your faith
    d)  Claim your victory.

2. Your reward for having faith is:
    a) You will become sons/daughters of God.
    b)  You will receive power to do mighty works.
    c)  You will receive perfect peace.
    d)  You will be kept safe and your prayers will be answered.

## Chapter One

### Prayer

Is there a problem or desire that you have prayed and hoped for, for so long you have given up on it? Have you pushed it to the back of your mind, saying this is an impossible situation? I just don't know what to do. I don't think this problem can be solved. Is there something in your life that's tormenting you and you feel it will never stop? So you stopped trying and you let it continue to happen, because you feel it's an impossible situation and it can't be corrected? Is there an unsaved family member, maybe a spouse or child whom you have given up on and tagged them as worthless, hopeless or impossible to deal with? Do you feel they can't be saved? Do these questions sound familiar to you? If they do you have picked the right book to read. It is not by chance that the Holy Spirit directed you to this little book.

*Matt.17:20 And Jesus said unto them. Because of your unbelief: for verily I say unto you, if ye have faith as a grain of mustard seed, ye shall say unto this mountain, Remove hence to yonder place; and it shall remove and nothing shall be impossible unto you.*

I am writing this book to let you know that there are no impossible situations when you have faith and you trust in God. You can barely see a mustard seed it is so tiny. When this seed is planted and watered it will grow into a big plant and produce a useful product. I know most Christians have heard the parable of the mustard seed many times. You are probably wondering what this has to do with the questions I asked in the beginning of this chapter. The questions asked earlier are common problems in people lives today. Unanswered prayers are sometimes directly or indirectly related to our faith and our patience. If you lend me your mind and your imagination until the end of this book I will share with you what the Holy Spirit put in my heart regarding planting a seed of faith, patience, prayer, tithing and getting prayer results.

*Mark 11:24 Therefore I say unto you, what things soever ye desire, when ye pray, believe that ye receive them, and ye shall have them.*

Let's think about this for a minute. If you pray for a special something you are releasing your faith. You are asking God for what you want or need, because you believe he can produce what you ask for. When we pray we are also planting a seed of faith. Faith is believing what you can't see. Just like a child who has all confidence in their father, will jump off a ladder into his arms because they believe without a doubt that he will catch them. Our faith in God is the same as that child's faith in their father. Are we not children in God's sight? We cannot pray and expect to receive an answer unless we have faith.

*Romans 12:3 God hath dealt to every man the measure of faith.*

No one can say they do not have faith. We exhibit faith in humans in machinery and the service they render us. Yet we consistently doubt God. Faith must be exercised. Faith can be tried and faith can be kept. We exercise faith by asking God through prayer for help. Our faith is tried by God through tests he allows us to go through. God will try our faith until we have overcome our fears and our dependence upon people and things. He will test us until we can put all confidence in him and in his ability to do and supply all things in our lives.

*1 John 5:14 And this is the confidence we have in Him that, if we ask any thing according to his will, he hearths us:*

We cannot pray to God for evil and expect to get an answer from Him. If you are praying for evil and get results be careful, the question is where your answer is coming from. The prince of darkness, the devil, deals in evil. We as Christians should not pray for evil. If we pray according to the Lord's teaching he will hear us and answer are prayer.

A new convert may not know how to pray. I will dedicate a couple of paragraphs on how to pray. First of all a prayer has no boundaries. It can be very small or gigantic. The size or amounts of words don't mean it will get answered any faster or slower. Sometimes prayer will be refused if it is not in accord with the divine will of God. Some prayers get answered faster because they are in the will of God and because of his mercy. In the bible there are scriptures in which short prayers were prayed and received answers.

*Ec 5:2 Be not rash with thou mouth, and let not thine heart be hasty to utter anything before God: for God is in heaven, and thou upon earth: Therefore let they words be few.*

*Mt. 6:7 But when you pray, use not vein repetitions, as the heathen do: for they think that they shall be heard for their much speaking.*

Do these scriptures lead us to believe that short prayers are better? When I prayed over these scriptures for understanding I received the following from the Holy Spirit. We are not to use prayer to bring attention to ourselves, or to try to appear holier than others. When we present a request to God in prayer, we should be careful how we present it. In my life experience I have prayed short prayers and received answers and long prayers and received answers. I have seen other Christians do the same.

There are several people in the bible that prayed for a purpose and received answers. Let us look at some of these prayers according to scripture. I will start with well known brief prayers. I will quote these prayers so you can see them and learn from their structure. One well known brief prayer is the prayer of Jabez. In this prayer Jabez is praying for a blessing from the Lord. And He received an answer.

*1Chr.4:10  And Jabez called on the God of Israel, saying, Oh that thou wouldest bless me indeed, and enlarge my coast, and that thine hand might be with me, and that thou wouldest keep me from evil, that it may not grieve me! And God granted him that which he requested.*

This was a very simple thorough to the point prayer. Jabez knew what he wanted and asked for it in few words. This prayer works I have used it with good results. The next prayer is not as shot as the prayer of Jabez it is a medium length prayer prayed by Hezekiah.

*Isaiah 38:1 In those days Hezekiah was sick unto death. And Isaiah the prophet the son of Amoz came unto him, and said unto him. Thus saith the Lord, Set thine house in order: for thou shalt die, and not live.*

*Isaiah 38:2 Then Hezekiah turned his face towards the wall, and prayed unto the Lord.*

*Isaiah38:3 And said remember now, O Lord, I beseech thee, how I have walked before thee in truth and with a perfect heart, and have done that which is good in thy sight. And*

*Hezekiah wept sore.*

The Lord heard Hezekiah's prayer and gave him 15 more years to live. Notice Hezekiah's prayer was simple and of few words. He did something different than Jabez, he cried and the Lord answered his prayer The next scripture is referring to Stephen's prayer for his murderers. Stephen is known as the first myrtle.

*Acts 7:59 And they stoned Stephen, calling upon God, and saying, Lord Jesus, receive my spirit.*

*Act 7:60 And he kneeled down, and cried with a loud voice, Lord, lay not this sin to their charge. And when he had said this, he fell asleep.*

We cannot forget the prayer of the thief on the cross next to Jesus. The Lord heard his prayer and saw his tears and blessed him.

*Luke 23:42 and he said unto Jesus, Lord, remember me when thou comets into thy kingdom.*

The most well know brief prayer is the prayer of Jesus on the cross asking for forgiveness for his murderers and when he commended his spirit to God.

*Luke 23:34 Then said Jesus, Father, forgive them; for they know not what they do.*

*Luke 23:46 And when Jesus had cried with a loud voice, he said, Father, into thy hands I commend my spirit: and having said thus, he gave up the ghost.*

These prayers were examples of brief prayers taken from scripture. These prayers were short to the point and powerful. Each prayer received an answer.

There are several notable prayers in the bible. Some of these prayers are very long and some are moderately long. They were offered up to request something from God and these prayers received answers. We will start with Jonah's prayer from the belly of the great fish.

Jonah was a prophet of God. He was summoned by God to go to the city of Nineveh and speak out against their sins. The city of Nineveh had a terrible reputation for its sin and corruptness. Most people were afraid to go into this city. Jonah did not want to go to Nineveh because he was afraid. He was disobedient and did not go to Nineveh. He took a boat to go in another direction. As a punishment for his disobedience, God caused Jonah to be thrown overboard by those sailing with him. God prepared a great fish in the water. The fish swallowed Jonah and he stayed in the belly of the fish for 3 days and 3 nights. While in the fish he prayed the following long prayer, and the fish vomited him up onto dry land.

*Jonah 2:2 I cried by reason of mine affliction unto the Lord, and he heard me; out of the belly of hell cried I, and thou heardest my voice.*

*Jonah 2:3 For thou has cast me unto the deep, in the midst of the sea; and the flood compassed me about: all thy billows and thy waves passed over me.*

7

*Jonah 2:4 Then I said I am cast out of thy sight; yet I will look again toward they holy temple.*

*Jonah 2:5 The waters compassed me about, even to the soul: the depth closed me round about, the weeds were wrapped about my head.*

*Jonah 2:6 I went down to the bottoms of the mountains; the earth with her bars was about me forever: yet hast thou brought up my life from corruption, O Lord my God.*

*Jonah 2:7 When my soul fainted within me I remembered the Lord; and my prayer came in unto thee, into thine holy temple.*

*Jonah 2:8 They that observe lying vanities forsake their own mercy.*

*Jonah 2:9 But I will sacrifice unto thee with the voice of thanksgiving, I will pay that I have vowed. Salvation is of the Lord.*

Jonah's prayer was a long prayer that got an answer. Jonah was released from his punishment alive. If you have not read the book of Jonah do so it teaches a strong lesson on obedience to God.

The following long prayer was prayed at the Pentecostal gathering after Jesus ascended to the Father. It was prayed by the multitude of believers that gathered there who were of one heart and one accord. This prayer is notable because after it was completed the gathering place called the, upper room, was shaken by the Holy Spirit. Everyone gathered there was filled with the Holy Spirit and spoke in tongues. This was the very first time so many had experienced the present of the Holy Spirit at one time.

*Act 4:24 And when they heard that, they lifted up their voice to God with one accord, and said, Lord, thou art God which hast made heaven, and earth, and the sea, and all that in them is:*

*Act 4:25 Who by the mouth of thy servant David hast said, Why did the heathen rage, and the people imagine vain things?*

*Act 4:26 The kings of the earth stood up, and the rulers were gathered together against the Lord, and against his Christ.*

*Act 4:27 For of a truth against thy holy child Jesus, whom thou hast anointed, both Herod and Pontius Pilate, with the gentiles, and the people of Israel, were gathered together,*

*Act 4:28 For to do whatsoever thy hand and counsel determined before to be done.*

*Act 4:29 And now, Lord, behold their threatenings: and grant unto thy servants, that with all boldness they may speak thy words.*

*Act 4:30 By stretching fort thine hand; to heal; and that signs and wonders my be done by the name of thy holy child Jesus.*

*Act 4:31 And when they had prayed, the place was shaken where they assembled together; and they were all filled with the Holy Ghost, and they spake the word of God with boldness.*

The next prayer is part of the Sermon on the Mount, and is called the Lord's Prayer or the Apostle's Prayer. It was given by Jesus as the way we should pray. This prayer also gets answers because God knows what we need before we ask and this is the way Jesus said for us to pray

*Matt. 6:9 After this manner therefore pray ye: Our Father which art in heaven, Hallowed be thy name.*

*Matt. 6:10 Thy kingdom come. Thy will be done in earth, as it is in heaven.*

*Matt. 6:11 Give us this day our daily bread.*

*Matt. 6:12 And forgive us our debts, as we forgive our debtors.*

*Matt. 6:13 And lead us not into temptation, but deliver us from evil: For thine is the kingdom, and the power, and the glory, forever A-men.*

So can we say that the length of the prayer does not matter as long as it is done in decency and order? When we pray if we use some basic steps we don't have to worry about getting a prayer through, we just have to be patient and wait on the Lord to answer us. The following steps I learned as a very young prayer worrier from an older prayer worrier. When I follow these steps I can get a prayer through.

## **Prayer Steps:**

1. Do not pray for show.
   a) Go into your secret place to pray so you can speak one to one with the Lord.
2. At the beginning of your prayer:
   a) Humble yourself before the Lord.
   b) Ask for forgiveness for your sins
   c) Praise him because he is God
   d) Thank him for all he has done for you.
3. Next ask him for what you want/need:
   a) At this point you want to be careful what you ask for,
   b) Make sure what you ask is in the divine will of God.
4. Ending:
   a) Thank him in advance for an answer.
   b) End with Amen.


There is always a question about how often one should pray for a given situation. It depends on where you are in your faith. If you need to pray frequently until you get an answer that's ok. If you are of great faith and only need to pray once that's ok. Do not condemn someone else because they do not pray at the same frequency as you do. Prayer and faith is an individual thing between the person and God. Is it wrong to pray in public or in church, if you are a prayer worrier or you are called on to do alter call? It is never wrong to pray for others. It is how you pray and your personal reason for the prayer. Remember God see and knows your heart. If your heart is pure and humble, and your prayers are honest God will bless you and answer your prayers. The following scriptures are in Jesus' own words.

*Matt 18:10 Two men went up into the temple to pray; the one a Pharisee, and the other a publican.*

*18:11 The Pharisee stood and prayed thus with himself, God I think thee, that I am not as other men are, extortioners, unjust, adulterers, or even as this publican.*

*18:12 I fast twice in the week, I give tithes of all that I possess.*

*18:13 And the publican, standing afar off, would not lift up so much as his eyes unto heaven, but smote upon his breast, saying, God be merciful to me a sinner.*

*18:14 I tell you, this man went down to his house justified rather than the other: for every one that exalteth himself shall be abased; and he that humbleth himself shall be exalted*

See why it is so very important to humble ourselves before praying. We do not want to be like the Pharisee all proud and bragging. The Lord will not answer our prayers in a puffed up (proud) state of mind. Now think of a problem you need

God to fix or give you an answer for. Now read Mark 11:24.

*Mark 11:24 What things so ever ye desire, when ye pray, believe that ye receive them and ye shall have them.*

Try putting the word I in each place ye appear. Repeat this scripture three times. Do you believe this scripture is true? If you do believe it is true then proceed on with this book. If you don't believe it is true I want you to ask yourself why you don't believe it, especially if you confess to be a Christian. Next I want to give you a task to complete before you continue on with this reading.

*Romans 10:17 So faith cometh by hearing, and hearing by the word of God.*

Spend some time in studying scriptures on faith and prayer. Then ask God through prayer to strengthen your faith and unbelief. Give yourself several days then come back to this book and continue. Why did I give those weak in faith a task? This is an action book the reader will learn by doing. Praying and studying the word will build faith in God in the Christian. As you study and pray it will grow you in patience. You will grow in faith. You will grow in studying and tithing. You will grow in your prayer life.

For those who believe Mark 11:24. Your next step is you are going to plant a seed of faith for a problem or a desire in your life. It can be something you have been praying for and given up on or a new problem or request. Make sure what you ask for is what you really want. There is an old saying be careful of what you pray for you just may get it. Do not pray for anything that's not of God. Your prayer will not be answered by God.

I want you to Keep in mind you are planting a supernatural seed. You are going to plant a seed of faith for whatever problem in your life or request you need an answer for. You will water that seed daily and watch it grow. Somewhere between today and six months from now or longer depending on God's will, someone reading this book will harvest the crop from that seed. Now take a sheet of paper write the problem or desire you thought of. Now speak the problem in your mind 3 times. Remember this is between you and God. You don't have to tell the world or all your friends what you are praying for. Keep it to yourself. God knows that's enough. Put the paper in your bible. I want you now to repeat this prayer out loud. If you are alone name the problem out loud, when you come to that part of the prayer. If you are with others say the problem or request in your mind and continue on. Before you pray make sure you can keep a promise you make to God. If you cannot keep a promise you make to God do not repeat this prayer until you are sure you can.

**Prayer:**

Lord I am planting a supernatural seed of faith today through prayer. I am asking you to take this request (name Problem or request) fix it, turn it around for the good of all concerned according to your will. Lord I will be careful to stay out of it and let you work. After you take it Lord I am going to water this seed with tithing, with prayer, with fasting and studying your word, until the harvest comes and you answer my prayer amen.

What did you just do? You gave God your problem/request. You planted a seed of faith. And you made a promise to God. Remember you can't buy God. So what was your promise? You promise to water your faith seed. How? With prayer, fasting, tithing and studying the word. You also promised to stay out of it and let God work the problem out. God will give the increase according to your labor. If your request is within the will of God you will be blessed.

*2 Corinthians 9:6: He which soweth sparingly shall reap sparingly; and he which soweth bountifully shall reap also bountifully.*

Depending on what we do after praying for God to help us with our problem/request, is directly related to our answer. If we give the problem to God and keep trying to handle it ourselves, we interfere with Gods work. Remember God will answer our prayers according to what is best for everyone. God sees the big picture while we only see what concerns us. You have now planted your seed of faith and gave the problem/request to God. You have stepped back to let God handle everything according to his will.

Next you will begin to water your seed of faith daily until harvest. Before your faith seed can grow and be harvested it will pass through 5 phases. God gave me these phases in a dream, after I had prayed over a problem I was having. I kept dreaming this dream periodically. Finally I asked God what to do with the information he gave me. He said write it, share it. He gave me an analogy of a seed to explain the phases to me and whoever I share this information with.

# Chapter 2

## Phase 1: The Incubation Phase

In this phase we recognize that we have a problem. We start to turn it over in our minds. Most people began to think or worry on it. Some may meditate or pray on the problem. As a Christian you go to the bible to find an answer. Something in the scripture stands out to confirm your direction, or God will send someone to witness to you or he may send you to someone.

This phase is where you plant your seed of faith. It simply mean you will give your problem to God through prayer, for him to solve it. The incubation phase can take one day to years. The important thing in this phase is you must be able to give the problem totally to God. You have to believe without a doubt that he will fix the problem. The incubation phase can be a very fragile time. Picture a real seed it is usually tiny and lifeless. You may not know what it will grow into at this point. When you first plant a seed it sits in the ground for a length of time and incubates or germinates. The seed is watered daily and it is fertilized as needed. This seed can either grow into something beautiful, which is a blessing and a miracle of God. Or it can sit in the ground and do nothing but decay. We can say, if it decays this is a stumbling block of the devil. Let us explore this a little farther.

Remember David the Sheppard boy. He loved the Lord with all his heart. The prophet was sent by God to David's father's house to anoint the future king which was David. At that time David had no idea what his future would be.

*1 Samuel 16:12 He sent and brought him in. Now he was ruddy and withal of a beautiful countenance and goodly to look to; and the Lord said arise anoint him for this is he.*

At that moment the seed of being King was planted into David's heart by the prophet Samuel. This seed incubated in David's heart, and it was nurtured until it bloomed and he became King. That's what you will be doing in the incubation phase. You will plant your faith seed through prayer. After you pray you will give the problem totally to God. You will then leave it alone. This is where faith comes in, we are suppose to nurture this seed until it blooms and is harvested. Depending on the amount of faith you have in God, will depend on how long you can leave this problem alone, or nurture it. As a general rule of human personality, doing this phase we struggle.

We as Christians have a tendency to give the problem to God then take it back and try to fix it. Usually because we become impatient and think God is moving too slow. Or we think he is not moving in the direction we want him to move. We may take it back and give it back to God several times before our faith kicks completely in and we can leave the problem alone.

*St Mark 11:24 Therefore I say unto you, what things soever ye desire, when ye pray, believe that ye receive them, and ye shall have them.*

Most Christians will pray then forget to start the fasting, studying the word and tithing right away (watering process). Remember the watering process must start immediately after the prayer request. This process strengthens us and helps us to leave the problem alone and let God work it out. Keep in mind the watering process is not busy work but building work. Once our faith gets stronger and we start to trust God more, then the watering process become automatic.

*Psalms 35:13 my clothing was sac cloth I humbled my soul with fasting and my prayer returned into mine own bosom.*

Prayer is the way we request what we desire from the Lord. When we water our seed of faith with fasting it humbles use so we can get our prayer through. In a humbled state there is nothing between us and God. We are saying to God by action that we are nothing and He is everything and we trust him totally with our need. When you fast, tell the Lord the date you will start and time. Also tell him your ending date and time. State if it will be a full fast without food or water or a partial fast with water or juice only. A fast can be from a few hours to days, it is between you and God and what you dedicate to him. You should start slowly if you are a first time faster. If you are on medications consult your doctor before starting a fast. As you become stronger at fasting you will be able to increase your length of fast time. Always listen to the Holy Spirit he will guide you through your fast.

*Romans 10:7 So then faith cometh by hearing and hearing by the word of God.*

When we water our seed of faith by studying the word daily we are keeping our mind on the Lord. We are surrounding ourselves with his teachings his words will comfort us. The more scripture we hear and read the stronger our faith becomes. The more we read the better we understand how Jesus would handle a similar situation and we began to use the teachings in our own life. The stronger our faith becomes the easier it is for us to wait on the Lord for an answer to our prayer. Remember the watering phase is a building phase.

# Chapter Three

## Phase 2: The Testing Phase

*James 1:3 knowing this that the trying of your faith worketh patience.*

Before a real seed can sprout or bloom and bring forth fruit it has to go through something. In the same respect before your prayer is answered you will go through something. No pain no gain. A real seed has to go through a change under the ground where we can't see it. When the seed is first planted it is dormant it has no life. As it is watered and nurtured it starts to swell. As the seed continues to be watered and fertilized it continues to swell and starts to develop roots which reach down into the soil. These roots anchors and stabilizes the seed, they are the way the plant will get water and nourishment.

After some time you can see an elevation in the dirt over the seed. At this time the grown is still closed. We can't see it but, there are changes going on under ground. With continued watering and sun and fertilizer, week's later cracks appear in the elevation of the soil. More weeks go by before a little green leaf will appear through the crack. The leaf will be so small you can hardly see it. Some days later a beautiful plant springs forward and starts to grow. The seed had to go through something before it became a plant. It had to go through rocks, dirt, smelly fertilizer, water, and heat from the sun. It even had to be protected from insects and other creatures that could destroy it. All these things happened to the seed before it turned to a viable plant, before it reaches harvest time.

*1 Peter 5:8 Be sober, be vigilant; because your adversary the devil, as a roaring lion, walketh about seeking whom he may devour.*

When we as Christians go through our problems and situations the devil is going to attack us and the Lord will allow him to attack us.

Picture this, the insects, rocks and other creatures in the soil which the seed had to get pass is just like the tricks and tactics the devil uses against us when we plant our seed of faith through prayer. His job is to deceive and to hinder us. He does this by keeping us bound to our fears and faults, and by attacking our faith. The real seed had the rocks, insects and other creatures to deal with. We have the devils tricks and attacks to deal with. He uses things like lying, deceit, false accusations, temptations, lust, strong drink, drugs, confusion, physical abuse, imprisonment, divorce, bad health, and alternative life styles. He will use anything and everything he can to make our problem seem overwhelming. His job is to try to make us give up. He wants to be the head of our life. The advisory will talk to you doing the testing phase. He will tell you all kinds of things. Like if the Lord was going to do something about your problem he would have done it by now. He will send your friends and your enemy with all kinds of accusations and gossip and gimmicks to side tract you.

*Psalm 37:5 commit they ways unto the Lord, trust also in him, he shall bring it to pass.*

You have to continue to trust in God at this time you can't give up or listen to the devil. The Lord has not forgotten you.

Doing the testing phase you have to water more. If you were praying 5 minutes increase it to 15 minutes, If 15 minutes increase to 30 minutes or an hour. Increase your fasting days. Increase your studying time. Surround yourself with more things that are of the Lord. Surround yourself especially with Christians that will encourage you and study and pray with you. Do not listen to the devil nor give him your time. Don't be afraid to stand up to the devil rebuke him in Jesus name and tell him to get behind you. Learn scripture so you can use them against the devils attacks. Whatever form he comes at you in, whether an enemy bringing negative words or an action against you, all you have to do is bombard him with spoken scripture and he will flee. You can speak the scripture out loud or to yourself.

*Proverbs 3:5-6 Trust in the Lord with all thine heart and lean not unto thine own understanding In all thy ways acknowledge him and he shall direct they path.*

Doing the testing phase the more you lean on God in faith the less the devil can trick you. When you get discouraged, fight it with prayer and scripture. Stay busy in the Lord, an idle mind is a mind the devil will use. A prayed up mind is a mind the devil can't abuse. Believe it or not while you are being tested God has started to work that problem out. The seed of faith is starting to get results. You just can't see it yet. Everything happens in God's time frame. Have faith and hold on.

# Chapter Four

## Phase 3: The Working/Investing Phase

*1 John 2:26 For as the body without the spirit is dead so faith without works is dead also.*

When you plant that seed of faith and believe that God will move that impossible problem, not only should you fast, pray, and pay your tithes, You must start to work in the ministry using your gift. Find out what your gift is and start to us that gift. Your gift can be the simplest thing. It can be standing at the door greeting people. Hugging someone daily saying God loves you. You can be the church janitor and keep the church clean. It could be helping the elderly in their homes. Your ministry doesn't have to be great but it has to be dedicated to God and in the will of God. Giving food and clothing to the hungry and homeless is a ministry. Give a dollar to that woman or man with the sign on the corner can be a ministry if you set aside a certain amount to give monthly or weekly. You will also have to dedicate your gift to God, as your ministry and be faithful in the work. Street witnessing is a ministry. Your gift may not seem great to people on earth but to God it is great, if it comes sincerely from your heart. You should work until your prayers are answered and even after they are answered. If you keep busy in the Lord, it keeps the devil from getting to you and leading you astray, while you wait for your prayer to be answered.

*1 Corinthians 15:58 Therefore my beloved  brethren, be ye steadfast, unmovable, always abounding in the work of the Lord, for as much as ye know that your labour is not in vain in the Lord.*

Most of us beg God from sun up to sun down twenty four seven. Even in our sleep we're probably asking for something. We cry crocodile tears with our hands out stretched, asking give me, heal me, deliver me, I need, why me. We expect God to supply what we ask for. If you are asking for something from God why not give back in some way.

When you are working in this phase you are not just working and waiting for an answer to your prayer, you are investing in your salvation. While investing in your salvation you will be helping Gods people. You are feeding His sheep. Remember a willing worker receives many blessings. Whatever you do for Christ will last, all of your efforts will not be in vain. Not only are you investing you will be defeating the devil by being steadfast and unmovable in your faith. If you stay strong in faith and stay strong in prayer and are busy for the Lord the devil can not hinder you.

# Chapter Five

## Phase 4: The Continuation Phase

In this phase you have to be very careful, because this is when your prayer starts to be answered. A portion of your prayer may be answered at this time. Notice I said a portion of your prayer. You may be thinking well if a portion of my prayers is answered why do I have to be careful? The answer is we as humans want instant gratification in everything. Sometimes the Lord bless in small increments, and not all at once. He blesses and then tests, blesses and then tests.

In phase 4 God may answer part of your prayer first. You being impatient take this as the full answer to your prayer. So you settle for less than God has for you. That's why this phase is dangerous. Let me give you an example. Say you are praying for your whole family to be saved. After some time of laboring at prayer and fasting one member accepts God and is saved. The other members seem not to care about being saved. If you accept this as the complete answer to your prayer the other family members will be lost. The devil will try to fool you in this phase by telling you; Oh well at least one came to Christ. You don't give up at this point. Where is your faith in God? Remember when a situation seems impossible that's when God is working it out. You planted a seed for the whole family. One got saved first, that's a partial answer.

Remember what I told you about the little seed. Picture the ground in your mind. What happens just before the plant springs up from the ground? There will usually be cracks in the dirt where the plant is trying to push through. Each seed grows at different speeds. One will come up first that's only part of what was planted. Other seeds are trying to push through the dirt and rocks and water and fertilizer that's why there are cracks in the dirt. Don't accept one plant as the full harvest

*Heb.11:1 state faith is the substance of things hoped for, the evidence of things not seen.*

So don't give up on what you can't see, keep your faith. Don't write off what you don't know or understand. If you prayed for the whole family thank God for that one save relative. Then you keep praying in faith, keep fasting and paying your tithes, keep working.

*Rom. 10:17 reads so then faith cometh by hearing and hearing by the word of God,*

Yes; you keep studying God's word. Yes, you have to keep paying your tithes, and yes keep working in the ministry. After sometime those other relatives will be saved also. Just like the seeds if given time the other seeds will push through the cracks in the soil and become

plants. Everything happens in God's time and according to his divine plan. Have faith for your total answer. Always be happy for the first fruit of the harvest. Be thankful for that one portion of your prayer that got answered.

*James 1:3 says knowing this, that the trying of your faith worketh patience.*

At this time we will also need patience to hold on and wait for God to grant the rest of our request. Always remember there is more to come. No matter how long it takes keep praying fasting, tithing and working. Our reward is only as great as our faith. Remember God's time is not our time.

*Mat.9:29 Jesus said according to your faith be it unto you.*

# Chapter Six

## Phase 5: The Gleaming Phase

*John 4:36 And he that reapeth receiveth wedges, and gathereth fruit unto life eternal; that both he that soweth and he that reapeth may rejoice together.*

This phase is harvest time. It takes time to work through a problem. Especially when the good of all concerned must be considered. God works in mysterious way. While you were praying and fasting for that problem your faith was strengthened. While you were praying for that situation God was changing your life.

Somewhere doing the process you began to take off the old man and put on the new man. In other words you started to change. While you were praying, God strengthened your faith; he strengthened your prayer life and your fasting ability. He even strengthened your ability to get into the word and study. He also taught you to tithe more freely. God changed your thinking process and you did not know it. While you were going through that problem and reading the word, you took on a new way of thinking. Scripture thoughts started to creep into your conscious mind. Thoughts like: Through God all things are possible. If I have faith the size of a mustard seed I can move mountain. He is my deliverance and strong tower. He is my rock and my fortress. Do you see what happened? As you watered you started to get rid of baggage. You cleaned your closet out, by praying, fasting, studying, working and tithing. You were able to rid yourself of some of those old skeletons that were hiding in the closet.

Hate can not dwell where there is love and compassion. Most definitely the devil cannot survive in love he has to flee. Not only did you change but the problem you were praying for started to be resolved. If you were praying for people their life started to change. Remember God answers prayers to benefit all involved. If you don't give up in phase 4 and take less than what God has for you, in phase 5 everything works out. In phase 4 you have to keep pressing in prayer. You have to stay strong in fasting. It is necessary to keep tithing and working. You must press on in faith and not give up. When phase 5 comes not only will your prayer be answered; you will have evolved into a stronger Christian. In phase 5 you can harvest the fruit of your labor.

Whatever you planted a seed for through God it is possible to fix. That broken marriage can be mended, because through God it is possible. That love one on drugs can be delivered because it's possible through God. That homeless situation can be resolved, because with God it's possible. That health problem can be healed, because with God it is possible. Your enemies can be concord, because it is possible with God. Problems with the children will get better through God it becomes possible. Abusive parents, wives, and husbands can become loving with God working it out. Whatever impossible problem you planted a seed for in the beginning of this reading will become possible over time. In phase 5 a change will be manifested in you and in the problem if you don't give up. You will be blessed and your prayers will be answered.

*Ps.126:5 They that sow in tears shall reap in joy.*

# *Chapter Seven*

## *Conclusion:*

To help the reader better understand the phases stated in this book I will present a fictional scenario a person may face in everyday life. The similarity of the characters in this scenario to anyone living or dead is purely coincidental. By reading this scenario the reader will be able to step back and look at their own problem and understand what phase they are in. Being able to identify the phase of your problem will help you to be patient and wait on the Lord for a full answer to your prayer.

### Incubation Phase:

Mrs. J.a wife discovers her husband Mr. is seeing another woman. The other woman is much younger than the husband and the wife. The wife is devastated. She has given her whole life to her husband and her children. The children are still young and need their father in the home.

She calls her best Faith, who is a believer in prayer, faith, fasting and tithing. The friend tells her they have to stand in prayer for her situation. Mrs. J. is not a strong believer she don't see how prayer can help her situation. She asked, her friend how can prayer help me? He is doing this of his own free will. She asked why God is letting him get away with it. The friend convinces the wife that they should meet and touch and agree in prayer regarding the problem. The wife reluctantly agrees. The two women met and entered into prayer regarding the problem. Then Faith tells Mrs. J. she has to give the situation totally to God and not try to fix it herself. She told Mrs. J. if at all possible try not to think about the problem. The friend suggested she set aside some time daily to study the word. The friend said she should start to study the word diligently especially when she starts to dwell on her husband and what he is doing. The friend reminded the wife that God will work the problem out for the good of all that are involved and in his own time. The friend told her she should find something in the ministry to do to keep her busy. She explained the importance of paying her tithes. She mentioned to the wife that she will have to wait on God and be patient for an answer.

## Testing Phase:

The wife was so depressed and angry she did not really want to put the energy into doing what her friend told her to do. She spent several weeks just moping around doing nothing much but crying and being verbally abusive to her husband and the children. The friend would call her or drop by regularly to check on her. The friend would point out scriptures for the wife to study that would increase her faith. To make sure she read the scriptures the friend would call and go over them with her and pray with her. She hoped this would get the wife motivated to start to study on her own. The friend would come and take her and her children to church. She would take her to participate in the ministry she chose as much as possible.

Mrs. J. would become very verbal about the bodily injury she wanted to afflict on her husband and the other women. She would sometimes follow her husband to see where he was going and what he was doing. Mr. J. remained unfaithful. He was becoming less and less discreet with his actions. The good thing was the children were too young to notice there was a problem between their mom and dad.

## Working and Investing Phase

Mrs. J. finally became motivated and became a faithful Christian. Without being prompted by her friend, Faith. She started to pray, fast, study the word, and pay her tithes. She continued to work in the ministry and began to like using her gift. It at least kept her mind off her problem. This was a big change for her because she never did anything consistently for the Lord before. Mrs. J. even got a part time job because her husband was not giving her as much money for the house anymore. The Job gave her a since of worth. Mrs. J's faith grew and she became a stronger Christian. Mrs. J. kept praying, studying the word, working in the ministry, and tithing. She kept her faith that God would work it out. In the mean time Mrs. J. came out of her deep depression. She lost that feeling of worthlessness she was harboring. She became a believer with unfaltering faith. Mrs. J. very seldom thought about her problem unless the devil caused her husband to abuse her.

Her husband continued to have the affair. He now stayed away from home over night and sometimes days at a time. When he was home he would be verbally abusive to Mrs. J. and indifferent to the children. The children knew their father as being caring and he always liked to do things with them. He no longer wanted to do anything with them.

## Continuation Phase:

One day after about 6 months Mrs. J. could not take the verbal abuse any longer, she stood up to Mr. J. She told him if he was so unhappy with her and the children then he could leave. She stated she would no longer take his abuse. She said she would rather he was out of the house paying child support and alimony than being there making everyone miserable. Mr. Jones was shocked. His wife had never stood up to him like that before. He changed his attitude. When he started to be abusive he would give it a second thought because there was a look that came into his wife's eyes that made him uneasy. Mr. J. continued with the affair but he became discreet again. He would come home late at night and not stay out all night.

Mrs. J. started to take the children on short trips over a weekend or a few days. These trips lifted their spirits. One weekend evening Mr. J. came home to find an empty house. He did not know where his family was. He called all the family members and friends with no avail. He sat home all weekend jumping every time the phone rang and with every knock on the door. Every time a car passed the house he ran to the window to see if it was his family. Mrs. J. returned with the children late Sunday evening. They were laughing and talking about the fun they had. When they saw Mr. J. they stopped laughing immediately. He jumped to his feet and asked her in a loud voice. Where were you? I was worried sick about the kids. Mrs. J. just stared at him and hurried the children off to bed.

The devil had Mr. J. so wrapped up and blinded by his sin he failed to see what was going on in his own home with his family. That weekend Mr. J. spent alone not knowing where his family was brought him to a rude awakening. He thought Mrs. J. was sadly waiting on him and would gladly welcome him back with open arms if his fling did not work out. What Mr. J. did not know was that the prayer of the righteous availeth much. As he sat alone he started to realize that his wife had changed. Not only had she changed her appearance but there was something in her personality that wasn't there before. He just could not put his finger on it. She seemed more independent and sure of herself. He had not been home enough lately to know his wife was working. He started to think maybe she was having an affair. Something was different and he was going to find out what it was. Mr. J. started to follow Mrs. J. When he could not follow her he hired someone to follow her for him. They were to repot her every move back to him. Mr. J. was determined to prove she was up to no good, as he put it, and she was not going to get away with it.

Mrs. J. told faith what happened. The friend was very happy. She told Mrs. J. she needs to decide if she could really forgive her husband and if she wants him back or not. Faith also told her she need to find away to set down and talk with her husband about his affair. She gave her scriptures on marriage to study and on forgiveness. Mrs. J. was excited to see what the scripture stated on marriage and divorce so she immediately started to study.

## Gleaming Phase:

Mrs. J. friend was amazed with her growth spiritually and her newly found dedication to her work in the ministry. She told Mrs. J. she will need to pray and study even more because her faith seed was about to be harvested. Mrs. J. studied the scriptures her friend gave her and she decided to forgive her husband and try to work their problem out. She decided he would have to come home by his own decision and turn from his sin first.

Mr. J. because of his guilt about his own sin was still having his wife followed trying to catch her in sin. To Mr. J. surprise he found out that his wife had a part time job which he did not know about. He found out she was attending church regularly. She was going to the Children's sports games which were his responsibility. He found out his wife and the children were laughing more and seemed to be having fund together. This made him feel really guilty and left out. He felt he was not a part of his children life and happiness any more. He started to feel even more guilt because he was taking time with the other women's children and not with his own. He started to wonder where and how did he get into this situation. One day he was happily married and had a beautiful family. Now he was in a situation that was against everything he once believed in. His wife and children didn't care if he was around or not. He had started to notice his friends seem to be kind of cold towards him lately. Mr. J. started to wonder how he could get things back to the way they were. He decided to sit down with his wife and have a talk with her. He made the decision to break it off with the other women immediately.

The other woman in this scenario Mrs. B. was also going through something at the same time. Because she was married she had started to feel guilty about her unfaithfulness to her husband. He was always out of town working and she seldom saw him on a regular basis. She ended up in an affair with Mr. J. because she gave into the temptation the devil put in front of her. Her husband was still coming home as much as possible. He never changed the way he treated her and the children. She had no doubt that he loved her but she was unsure about how she felt about him. Mrs. B and Mr. B. were not saved and had never read the scriptures.

One weekend her husband came home excited about his newly found interest. He was telling her how one of his co-workers had invited him to church. He told her he had enjoyed the message and for something to do one evening a week he would go to bible study with his co-worker. Mr. B. brought a bible home with him and went over the lesson with Mrs. B. from the pass week. The lesson was on adultery and fornication. The lesson started her to feel guilty about her affair with Mr. J. The next week when her husband came home, he shared the pass week's lesson with her. The lesson was on forgiveness. Mrs.

B. started to feel somebody was trying to tell her something. Her husband encouraged her to try going to church and he helped her to find a church in their neighborhood. She agreed she would go when she had time.

Mrs. B. never went to the church and she continued to pretend to be listening to her husband's bible lessons when he came home. She kept wondering why he was pushing this on her. One very warm mid morning she took her children to the park. Mr. J. had not come by for several weeks now and she had nothing to do. At the park a lady approached her and asked if she could sit next to her so she could have a better view of her own children, playing. Mrs. B. stated it was ok.

The lady introduced herself as Faith; Mrs. B. introduced herself to the stranger not knowing the stranger was Mrs. J's friend. Faith being a person who loved to witness started a general conversation with Mrs. B. While talking to Mrs. B. Faith could sense a deep sadness in her. Faith turned to her and looked her in the eyes and smiled. She stated whatever your sadness is Jesus loves you and he will not forsake you. All you have to do is talk to him. Mrs. B. looked at her with a bewilder expression on her face. She said talk to him? Faith said yes just like we are talking now. She could see anger starting to appear on Mrs. B's face so she excused herself and gathered her children. As she left she called back glad to meet you. I will keep you in my prayers. Mrs. B. was thinking the nerve of that woman she don't know me. I did not ask her to pray for me. Then she murmured how did she know that I am sad. Faith went back to the park several times but she did not see Mrs. B. As Faith promised she kept Mrs. B. in her prayers. Mrs. B's. Husband continued to bring the pass week's bible study home with excitement and would go over the lesson with her.

One week Mr. B, read John 3:16 to her. For God so loved the world that he gave his only begotten Son; that who so ever believeth in him should not perish, but have everlasting life. Mrs. B. thought about the lady, Faith, in the park. She thought maybe there is something to this bible. She started to listen more carefully to Mr. B's lessons. As she listen she notice her sadness started to leave. She did not understand everything he said to her so she decided to try and read the words for herself. Mr. B showed her how to find the books in the bible and how to use the references.

Mrs. B decided to take the children back to the park one day because they had not been for a long time. She took her bible with her because she felt this was a good time to study. To her surprise Faith was in the park with her children. Faith greeted her cheerfully and came to set by her. Faith noticed the bible and asked was she a Christian. Mrs. B stated no I just became interested in the bible from my husband. He just started to study the word a few weeks ago. Faith smiled and told her she was a Christian. She told Mrs. B. they could study together when they met at the park.

Faith said she had her bible in the car and could start today. Mrs. B. stated she would like that.

As she studied with her husband and in the park with Faith she grew in faith and understanding of her sin with Mr. J. She asked for forgiveness from the Lord and decided to have a talk with Mr. J. Mr. J. had been trying to get his nerve up to go and talk to Mrs. B. also. One day he got out of bed and went straight to Mrs. B's house before he lost his courage. When he knocked on the door he prayed that the Lord would let her understand that their relationship could not go on. When Mrs. B. opened the door she was surprised to see him. She asked him to come in. When he sat down they both started to talk at the same time. He decided to let Mrs. B go first. She told him about her newly found interest in the Lord and what she learned from studying the word. She stated that it was wrong for them to be together. Mr. J breathes a sigh of relief. He said he had been feeling very guilty about what they did. Mr. J told Mrs. B, He and his wife had reconciled and he came to let her know. They talked for a long time and parted friends.

When you plant a seed of faith through prayer and you have patience to wait on the Lord for an answer you will be blessed. Remember When God answers your prayer things will be worked out for the good of all concerned.

## Scripture Reference

**The following scriptures were taken from the King James Version of the Bible.**

*Heb. 11:6 But without faith it is impossible to please him; for he that cometh to God must believe that he is, and that he is a rewarder of them that diligently seek him.*

*Heb. 10:35 Cast not away therefore your confidence, which hath great recompence of reward.*

*James 1:3 knowing this that the trying of your faith worketh patience.*

*1John 3:22 And what so ever we ask, we receive of him, because we keep his commandments and do those things that are pleasing in his sight*

*Eph. 6:13 Wherefore take unto you the whole armour of God, that ye may be able to withstand in the evil day*

*Eph. 6:16 Above all, taking the shield of faith, wherewith ye shall be able to quench all the fiery darts of the wicket*

*Mk 11:24 Therefore I say unto you, what things soever ye desire, when ye pray, believe that ye receive them, and ye shall have them*

*Mt. 6:7-8 But when ye pray, use not vain repetitions, as the heathen do; for they think that they shall be heard for their much speaking. Be not ye therefore like unto them: for your father knoweth what things ye have need of, before ye ask him.*

*Ja 5:13 Is any among you afflicted? Let him pray. Is any merry? Let him sing psalms.*

*Mt. 6:16 more over when ye fast, be not, as the hypocrites, of a sad countenance: for they disfigure their faces that they may appear unto men to fast.  Verily I say unto you, They have their reward.*

*Ps. 35:13 But as for me, when they were sick, my clothing was sackcloth: I humbled my soul with fasting; and my prayer returned into mine own bosom.*

*Matthew 7:7-8 Ask and it shall be given you; seek, and ye shall find; knock and it shall be opened unto you. For everyone that asketh receiveth; he who seeketh findeth; and to him that knocketh it shall be opened*

**The following scriptures were taken from the New International Version of the Bible**

*Matthew 21:22 If you believe, you will receive whatever you ask for in prayer.*

*Isaiah 30:19 How gracious he will be when you cry for help! As soon as he hears, he will answer you.*

*1 John 5:14-15 This is the confidence we have in approaching God: that if we ask anything according to his will, he hears us. And if we know that he hears us-whatever we ask – we know that we have what we asked of him.*

*Isaiah 65:24 Before them call I will answer: while they are still speaking I will hear.*

*John 15:7 If you remain in me and my word remains in you, ask whatever you wish and it will be given to you*

*Proverbs15:29 The Lord is far from the wicket but he hears the prayer of the righteous.*